Getting All T Handle

A Beginners Anal Sex Guide For

Painless Butt Sex

Brandee Lee

Table of Contents

Chapter 1…Introduction To Anal Play

Chapter 2…Should You have Anal Sex At All

Chapter 3…Anal Fingering Techniques

Chapter 4…. Anal Sex Positions

Chapter 5…"Just Relax Honey" is easier said than done.

Chapter 6…Anal Sex Techniques & Tricks

Chapter 7…Getting Yourself Ready To Take A Cock

Chapter 8… Analingus Is The Real Love Kiss

Chapter 9…The Best For Men Is Anal Prostate Stimulation

An Anal Evening With Brandee Lee

Chapter 1

Introduction To Anal Play

This book is for all of you who have wondered or even been a little curious about anal play and how to do it without having extreme pain.

I'm sure that you've already heard the jokes that end something like this "If anal sex is a pain in the ass, then you're probably doing it wrong". But the truth is anal intercourse should not really be extremely painful for the lady. If it is quite painful it's because of a lack of preparation and that probably is the single biggest turn-off for many women. Most of the lady's pain during anal intercourse is at the beginning with the head popping through the rings!

A typical couple begins with this type of anal scenario. It probably goes something like this. The couple is young and want to explore the dark and taboo side a little in their sexual relationship. So, they decide to make an attempt at anal intercourse. But unfortunately, they don't have a clue what they are doing, and they are not really fully prepared for it. So he carefully gets behind her and tries his best to push his cock into her anus without much warning or lubrication. She screams in shock and agony and ends up throwing herself away from the offending member that is causing her so much pain in her ass as her head hits on the headboard. That's the end of anal sex for her and in their relationship. I was lucky in my relationship that I married young, that is in my early twenties and didn't have any terrible negative anal experiences to turn me off.

But the truth is with proper preparations from a loving, caring man who you truly trust, anal intercourse can not only be as safe as any other kind of sex, but at least as enjoyable if not much more enjoyable, than regular intercourse. My husband absolutely loves the tightness of my ass and I love the really full feeling that his thick cock gives me. I told him the other day that I would truly let him fuck my ass everyday of our life if I didn't have hemorrhoids from having children and bearing down to give natural birth. The fact is the anus can be a very pleasureful erogenous zone because it contains more nerve endings than any other part of the body, except for the women's clitoris of course. With that being said, I will also throw in my usual, you know, this doesn't necessarily work for everyone, comment. Some couples will find it really enjoyable, and others will not.

Some people get all hung up on the "you're not sticking that big thing in there" mentality. We have been so thoroughly and culturally conditioned to believe that touching our anus is a bad taboo. So never mind actually playing with it on purpose. I mean that would probably be unheard of. I must confess that many years ago you would not have been able to convince me that I would ever have anal intercourse much less like it like I do. And I do have to admit now that I love my husband fucking my ass or burying a lubed finger in my asshole while his is pumping my G-spot with his hand.   In fact I love it so much it is now a regular part of our sex life when we can do it.

There is no necessary medical reason for the perceived taboo against anal intercourse. If we are being truly honest with ourselves the idea of doing something we're not supposed to do is really kind of exciting, isn't it?

The truth is If you practice good hygiene there isn't anything repulsive at all about it. It is also a good idea to make sure that you've gone to the bathroom and emptied out really good a couple hours prior to commencing your anal action. If you desire, you can also use an enema to clean out and be confident that you are clean. But it isn't really necessary. Although I will admit it does give you a peace of mind. My husband and I often both take an enema before we have a night of anal action together. We both love to eat each other's asses and it just makes it a little cleaner for us. If you're really worried, hop in the shower together and lather each other up really good and personally clean each other's private holes and then you can be assured that everything down there is as clean as it can possibly be. Besides cleaning someone else's butt hole can really act the erotic action.

At first when you are just starting out you should consider being extra careful by using a lubed-up condom for any anal intercourse play. Many couples will always use a condom for anal intercourse anyway. It makes the cock really slide in the anus a lot smoother. Especially if you want to go from anal sex to vaginal sex during the fun. All you have to do is pull the condom off his penis and have at it. The bacteria that lives in your rectum can really create havoc for her if they take up residence in your lady's vaginal canal.

I have a confession I must make from the start of this book: I absolutely love any kind of anal play. Even though it took us over twenty-five years of marriage, before I was even willing to try it. At first, anal was something that made me curious because of the domination aspect of it. But over the past few years, I've just really started to enjoy it. I mean enjoy it a lot.

In this chapter, I wanted to just talk about anal a little, to help you out if you're new to it. This is a book about anal sex for beginners that I wish I had read when I was a newbie to it.

If you want, you can skip to the last chapter and read an amazing story that's is a scenario of what most women wish would happen to them. But just to let you know it is a true story that actually happened to me. I caution you it is a little erotic and that's why it's the last chapter so you can skip it if erotic stories offend you.

Chapter 2

Should You Have Anal Sex At All?

The answer is quite a simple answer, yes…IF you really want to. But you shouldn't feel pressured to have anal sex or do any kind of anal stimulation if you aren't ready for it or aren't interested in it. There are tons of other ways to give pleasure to your partner other than anal play.

But the truth is anal sex can feel awesome whether you're a male or a female. I'm of course a female, so keep that in mind as you read the rest of this chapter. I'm telling this opinion from a girl's perspective. You may be asking yourself what does Anal Sex actually feel like? Just think about this for a minute, this is a much smaller hole that isn't really genetically designed for sex. So, with that being said it's going to be a lot tighter than your pussy.

Even if you're getting fucked by a relatively small penis you can still feel the pressure. But trust me sister if you'll let it, that is your anus it will actually stretch to fit around any penis size. Just think of the size of some of the bowel moments you have had in the past and how large they were. You looked in the toilet and couldn't believe that thing came out of you But unfortunately, unlike your pussy, it isn't going to be primed and ready to go no matter how horny or turned on you are. So, your man will have to learn to go slow at first.

If I had to choose a word there is one word, I can use it to best describe it: PRESSURE. Anal sex can really hurt if it is done improperly without any lube. Sometimes it's a pretty uncomfortable feeling at first, and when you go too quickly, the skin around your anus can actually tear a little. So, if it hurts and believe me, I'm not talking about just it feels a little uncomfortable, but actually hurts, you should pause and re-evaluate what's actually going on. Do you need to add more lube? Do you need to go much slower? Do you need to change positions and try one that has less pressure? Make sure you're trying anal with a lover who respects you so that he'll stop if it hurts you.

This is not the thing to try on a one-night stand my friend. I don't care what the erotica novels say. It took me and my husband quite a while and lots of tries before I could take actually his whole cock up my ass. I would get so tight he couldn't even get his cock to start going in my puckered hole. Then many times he would get soft as he tried to get it into my tight ring. It takes a really good hard on to do anal sex. Finally, after many tries, and a few months of anal play we made it happen.

Never forget this one main thing about making it quite painless. Anal sex requires lots of lube. Yes, you really need lots of lube? A good rule to follow is when you think you have too much lube, just add a little more for good measure.

When most women get really turned on, their pussy starts secreting a liquid and she gets really wet. Of course, some women get wetter than others. But this does not happen with your asshole, no matter how hot and heavy things get in the bedroom. So yes sister, you really do need lots of lube. Otherwise, your man's cock isn't going to slide in very easily and it WILL hurt, and that is hurt a lot. So yes, you absolutely need to use lots and lots of anal lube to get going.

I recommend picking up a lube that is made specifically for anal sex. My absolute favorite is ID Glide Anal Lube which retails for under $10. I'm one of those women that gets really super wet, but if my guy is fucking my pussy and then goes for the ass, it still isn't enough. Spit isn't enough either, I don't care what the erotic novels say. Don't skimp on using real lube – it makes all the difference in the world when it comes to pain in anal sex.

Chapter 3

Anal Fingering Techniques

How To Introduce Your Lover To Anal Play

Anal fingering can be a great way to introduce some new sensations into your sexual repertoire in your marriage. In fact, this is what turned me on so much to anal play. Once while my husband was going down on me, he stuck his finger into my asshole just as I was cumming and I almost passed out from the pleasure it brought me. The anus is totally packed with tons of pleasurable nerve endings, but I don't have to tell you that, you've probably had some pleasure when you went to the bathroom a time or two. But on the flipside, many of those nerve endings produce pain as well. Anal fingering can be extremely pleasurable or painful if you don't do it right. If you've never tried it before?

Here's how to make it really pleasurable for your lover.

First make sure to use plenty of lube both on the inside and outside of the anus area.

You may already know this, but there's no mistaking the importance that using a good amount of lube and what it does for anal sex. Or any other kind of anal play for that matter, including fingering. Don't try to use your spit, saliva, or pussy juice as a lube like you read in the erotic stories. Trust me sister, it's just not going to work. Instead, make sure you have a bottle of water based or silicone-based lubricant on hand before you ever get started. Use these lubes if you intend on using a condom or latex glove. Otherwise, good old Vaseline works quite well.

A scented lube can work really well for anal fingering, because not only do they work well, but they also smell great too. We like a cherry scented anal lube that makes the anal area smell like cherries. Your lover may be apprehensive that they will smell bad if you're that close to their most private hole, but if they've showered first and if you use a scented lube, it most likely won't be an issue at all.

Never use any of those desensitizing lubes when engaging in anal play. While it may seem beneficial to make sure your lover can't feel it as much, that also means you can do more damage to them than you intended to and not have any clue that you're doing it to her! Your lover will probably wake up in the morning sore or bleeding and won't ever want to try it again!

You should just start with one finger to probe with then move on to more after she becomes more stretched. And it may take a few different times to get her stretched enough to handle a whole finger or multiple fingers. This may seem like a no-brainer to you, but many people get so excited to try anal fingering with their lover that they try to use more than one finger to start off with. This won't work very well and may cause intense pain or discomfort. Always remember with anal play, it's a cinch by the inch and hard by the yard. It's important to start with just one finger, probably your pinky finger if your hands are extremely large like my husbands are. If they are thick like my husband's size 16 ring finger. Do this careful play at least until your lover gets used to the new sensation. Once your lover seems to be enjoying it and is well lubed up really good, you can work on introducing more fingers, one at a time.

You might also try to give them oral sex first – and even add this during your anal play.

For your lover to truly enjoy the amazing fingering sensations you're giving her during your anal fingering session, they have to be really, really turned on first. Even with plenty of lube, you're still going to have a difficult time inserting your finger if her anal muscles are too tight and not relaxed.

I know this for a fact, when I first started being anally penetrated with a penis by my husband, I had such a hard time relaxing and loosening up. My patient husband couldn't even get his cock head in me because I was so tight from tension. I so wanted him to penetrate me with that thick penis of his but for some reason I just couldn't relax. But once I had cum about five times from him eating my clit and thumbing and finger fucking my pussy, he took his lubed finger and shoved it all the way up my ass to his wrist. I was so turned on he took a medium sized butt plug and fucked me with it until I filled his palm with about an inch of cum.

So please whatever you do my friend always take the time that is necessary to get them really turned on first before you penetrate her with anything. Either through some form of foreplay or intense cunnilingus or fellatio for the men. Oral sex is always an excellent precursor to anal fingering, simply because it is such a great erotic activity. I remember again my husband had me so turned on with his tongue that by the time he finally inserted a butt plug into my ass and was fucking me with it, I was squirting my love juice in his face, something I had never done before, ever...So yes anal play made me into a true squirter.

So, lube your finger up really good and slip it slowly into your lover's anus while you're performing cunnilingus on them. They will be more apt to enjoy the feeling than shy away from it. Simply because what you were doing before already felt so good!

I would highly recommend to start that you would wear rubber or latex gloves or a finger cot when you are anal fingering your wife. It may make you feel a little awkward at first but believe me your lover will appreciate it. You may think you have your nails trimmed and your cuticles cut, but if your hands are at all callused as many men's hands are, that is you do work for a living, then your fingers are going to hurt your lover's tender anal canal. Ladies, with acrylic nails can also hurt their man when they're trying to massage their man's walnut sized prostate gland that is located just inside his rectum!

So just invest in a good box of gloves and keep them around the bed for using during anal fingering. Your fingers will actually go in much more smoothly, especially with enough anal lube on your finger. Also, it will protect you from getting bacteria or solid waste under your fingernails! Just be aware that if you use petroleum jelly or oil-based products they will break down condoms and of course latex gloves!

Rule Number Two is Simply Go Really Slow!

When you're first starting out fingering your lover's asshole, don't be tempted to go too fast. It's easy to go too fast and not even realize it when you're excited. But you can really hurt your lover this way. Instead, take your time and go really slow. Maybe as we've already said, build up your lover's pleasure with oral sex while you tenderly massage their anus. Even if you can only slowly get one finger in and out once, you're doing good for your first time. It takes time sister!

For most of the people who are starting out you may not even get to have a really amazing sex session the first time you try anal fingering with your lover. I didn't at least. So, your first time may actually be just "trying" it. Your lover isn't sure what to expect and they don't know what it's going to feel like. The first time might simply be them getting accustomed to what it's like. The next few times you'll notice your lover getting more and more into it, as they get used to how it feels, and they learn how to get pleasure out of it.

Then Simply Use A "Come Hither" Motion

Anal fingering is much the same as vaginal fingering. You want to slowly insert the finger, palm side up. Once you get into position, slowly move your finger in a "come hither" motion, as though you would if you were trying to stimulate her G-spot. This is really pleasurable for a woman, and even more so for a man, because it stimulates his walnut sized prostate gland.

Many people make the terrible mistake of thinking anal fingering is pushing the finger in and out of the anus with a pumping action. This is not going to be pleasurable at all! In fact, insertion and pushing past the tight sphincter muscles is actually the most painful part and only when it's over can the recipient actually begin to experience pleasure. If you're just pushing your finger in and out, you're just repeating the worst part of anal fingering over and over again.

Instead, simply use the come-hither motion to gently massage all the nerve endings on the inside of the anus and try to put some pressure on the pelvic floor. Combined this action with a glove, a lot of patience, and plenty of lube, you can get your lover to really enjoy anal fingering.

Chapter 4

Anal Sex Positions

It's important for your pleasure's sake that you totally understand all the important facts about positioning yourself to receive great anal sex from your mate. Listen to me, positions really matter in how it feels. Although for sure every situation is going to be a little different, based on your specific ass and the actual curve of your man's cock.

For my husband and I, we find that the doggie or spooning position works best for us. With bigger guys, spooning is also a good option, and if he has a strong upward curve, it works well to be in a kind of kneeling on the edge of the bed or a couch with him behind you. Almost every single guy for sure will get the positioning wrong at first, so you'll have to guide him most likely. I've personally found that my husband seems to aim too high. So, you must be in control. Sometimes this can be a little hard at first with all the lube that you have down there, but once he pops in place and you're really stretched good, he can take you over and over again. Nothing is more frustrating than you being ready to have him fuck your ass and can't seem to get in correctly. My husband had the problem of him going soft before he could get it in because I was so tight, I wouldn't let his cock inside. His cock has to be rock hard to enter into a woman's tight asshole.

A Great First-Time Position To Try

Now we can get into some of the really fun stuff before I give you some more techniques... positions, positions, positions……. Your positions should only be limited by your physical ability to get in and out of them and by what feels comfortable for the both of you at the time. Some positions will work wonderfully for some couples and not for others. It's entirely up to you to determine which ones work best for you. I will give you a few suggestions to start with and get your whistle wetted.

The first one and probably the most important one in my mind, simply is with the woman on top facing toward the man. Cowgirl it is sometimes called. I say it's the most important, because if it's your first time experiencing anal sex. This position will allow you to have total control of the insertion of his penis into your ass. This was what I used for my first anal experience, and I felt comfortable because I had the control over how far his penis was going in my ass or not going in.

I could stop when I felt I needed time to adjust to the burning sensation and then continue when it subsided and I felt ready to. It's mostly like when your passing a large bowel movement and you have that burning sensation at first and then once it's past the resistance, it feels really good. This is still my all-time favorite position for us, although reverse cowgirl and doggie work well for us to.

Ladies, all you need to do is to straddle your man facing toward him. Make sure that you've got lots of lubricant applied to his penis and to your ass. If there is one thing you never want to forget when it comes to anal sex is, too much lubricant is your best friend. You want to be able to have his penis slide in really smoothly with no friction at all.

Carefully grasp his penis firmly and position the head of his cock at the opening of your anus. Hold it in place while you gently push your ass down against it. It will move fairly smoothly for the first little bit and then you are going to encounter some real tight resistance. This is where the muscular ring protecting your asshole from staying open is. To get past this point, you really need to relax and breath. I know it's easy to say and hard to do, but you really have to try to relax and push down gently until you feel it pop past that first muscle. Now, you might want to take a minute here to absorb how it feels so far. Usually it will be a real hot burning sensation for most people. You may feel like you're going to want to drop a load. This is a normal feeling sister, and you won't actually crap yourself.

It has been suggested that breathing plays a very big role in successful anal intercourse. Just like in a woman's childbirth experience she will have a much easier time of it if she controls her breathing. If the woman silently takes a deep breath and then exhales slowly during the initial penetration of his cock it makes the act more pleasurable for both partners. It's like a tight pressing down feeling and sometimes if you push out while going down like you are having a bowel movement it will actually suck his cock deeper in your ass quickly.

Once you've adjusted to the penetration, try pressing down a little further on his penis, taking more inside your ass. This is a good time for your husband to play with your breasts, while you stroke and play with your pussy and clit with your fingers or a vibrator or whatever else works for turning you on. Never forget that anal sex is more exciting and pleasurable for the woman the more sexually turned on and excited you are because the less attention you are going to pay to any discomfort you might feel.

Then finally after it's in you can start moving up and down on his penis, letting it slide in and out of your ass. From this position you are in complete control and can wiggle side to side or move up and down as slow or as fast as you'd like. You can also control the depth and force of his penetration. If he pumps up and you can raise up and control things.

When you're comfortable with this movement and full feeling, you may also allow your partner to become more of a participant instead of having him remain passive and sit still. It's all up to you and ladies I don't think that he's going to argue too much, especially if this is something that he's been wanting to do and is finally getting the opportunity to experience it with you.

Other Positions You Might Want To Try

Here are some other positions that you can try out to see what you like best.

Doggie Style

This position works so well for regular vaginal intercourse that makes it also a good choice for anal intercourse as well. Just kneel on your knees and elbows on the bed or couch, remembering to relax your ass and breathe deeply as I told you. Your man then kneels directly behind your ass, facing towards you. He can hold your hips for stability. He will then bend forward guiding his penis into your anus opening and gently pushes it inside as you push back into him.

Entry is also made easier if you try to draw his penis into your ass as he is pushing forward. Your lover can then move his penis around inside your ass by thrusting his hips forward and backward, while you either remain still or move your hips from side to side. This position is also so great for deep penetration because it allows for fairly easy and deep penetration.

Full Front Her Legs Raised

In this awesome position the woman lies on her back and pulls her knees up as close to her chest as she can manage and then rests her feet on her partner's shoulders. The standing man then pushes down on her face to face. Sometimes it's good for a pillow or a wedge to be inserted under the woman's pelvis to raise it higher up for easier penetration. We have a liberator wedge that I must say is pretty awesome for penetration and less pressure on your back. You can also use a neck sling that goes around your neck to hold your legs up as well. The man can also push the woman's feet up over her head if he likes and she can do it. This position allows for easy and great deep penetration.

I used to put my toes in the headboard rail to hold me up for him.

Standing Up Position

In this standing position both partners are up standing facing the same direction. The woman can then bend over at the waist if she wants to. It is a good idea to use a wall or chair or something else for support against his thrusts from behind. This can also be accomplished from a kneeling position on the edge of the bed with him behind you. Depending on the height difference between you and your husband some adjustments may need to be made. This position does not work at all for us as I'm 5'4" and he is 6' tall. It works when I bend over but standing up is out of the question. This position is a convenient one for outdoor use and allows easy penetration and full movement provided there is something solid to hang on to.

Her Flat on Her Stomach

In this position, have the woman lying flat on her stomach. I like to use a pillow to raise my hips up a little for easy access and penetration. This allows the woman to relax more fully, and her hands are free to rub her clit or squeeze her breasts or do whatever she likes. Since the man will lay on top of the woman, he can also be more relaxed and have freer hand movements as well to grab her tits or to grab her hair and pull it back as he thrusts forward. The penetration in this position is not as easily accomplished and thrusting is also more difficult for some women. The woman is also fairly restricted in her movement. It is a great position for a little Analingus actions as well.

Both Are Laying Side by Side or Spooning

It's easy to casually switch from the position above. Both partners can fairly easily roll over onto their sides, with both facing the same way, with her drawing one leg up. This position allows for greater relaxation of your bodies and your hands are free to explore and caress each other's nakedness. Entry in this position is easy and penetration is fairly deep for this position. I personally love the full feeling my husband gives me from this position. Movement and thrusting can be rather limited at first, although we have found that vigorous thrusting is possible once you get used to the posture of the position.

The Couple Laying Side by Side – Facing Together

This is another variation to the two previous positions. In this particular position, the lovers are lying on their sides and are facing one another. The man must extend his pelvis in between the woman's bent legs. This position allows for deep entry, and the hands are free for any type of exploration. This position is also a little more intimate and allows for kissing and eye contact to take place while she is receiving a good ass fucking. Movement is fairly easy once insertion is made.

Chapter 5

"Just Relax Honey" Is Easier Said Than Done.

I'm sure that you've heard that statement from your husband before. He knows that in order for you to have anal sex with him, you have to relax so his cock can gain its entry. That always makes me laugh a little. Yeah, sure, it's really easy to relax when someone is trying to shove a cock up your butt.

Here's how I do it: first, I *breathe*. Yep, when you slowly breathe out, it gives the body an illusion of relaxing. That's why expecting mothers work on breathing properly during labor. So please by all means don't hold your breath! Let it out slowly to try to relax a little before his insertion. Next, do your best to clench your asshole a little. I know, it really seems counter-productive, but clenching it for a few seconds as hard as you can, and then letting it go. That's the moment he can more easily slip into your tight ass. Especially if you try to push like you are going to the bathroom as he is inserting his cock into your ass. It will work backwards and sometimes suck his cock into your tight orifice.

It also really helps to have your guy anally play with you a little with a finger first to stretch you out. I found that wearing butt plugs a couples hours before the action stretches me out good for his insertion. This gets your ass prepped for something bigger and helps you mentally relax as well. If you wear a butt plug around the house for a while, every time you move you will feel it and get turned on. I've had many orgasms just from wearing a butt plug and waiting for the big even that night. We're often not relaxed enough, because we're worried about pain and discomfort, so a little anal play with a finger or butt plug first does wonders to stretch you out.

Chapter 6

Anal Sex Techniques & Tricks

Some guys needlessly worry that liking anal sex or having their wife penetrate them with a dildo or finger makes them gay!

Nope sir. Being attracted to men makes you a homosexual or bisexual. Not having your sexy wife penetrating your ass with a finger or dildo. If you like it when your wife fingers your ass or uses a toy/or dildo on you, you aren't gay.

Actually, if the truth is to be known anal sex feels really good for most men because that's how your prostate gland can be stimulated from the inside. It also can't "turn" you gay if you have a lot of anal sex with your wife or solo. It just feels really good, and my husband has some of his best orgasms when I am using a vibrator on his ass.

Now you may be sitting there wondering what about having his cum in your ass.

Yes, it can be a bit uncomfortable at times. Seriously. I know, it feels good when it happens. I love the feeling of his cock pulsating as it is shooting cum deep in my ass, but afterwards, it's a little gross because that cum has to get out of there somehow. It's not very graceful, either. Having cum in my ass actually feels a little weird so sometimes I ask for him to pull out and cum on me or wear a condom.

It's not the end of the world, though. If you're fluid-bonded, try it with the man of your dreams. Now you might have a different experience than some women do. Just be prepared to gracefully excuse yourself to the restroom afterward so you can discharge that cum.

Absolutely Never Forget About Anal Safety

Also, I want to take some time to go over a few safety tips with you. If you're going to have anal sex, you need to know a few things before you get down and dirty into it.

First do not go from pussy to anal and then back to pussy with your cock. No matter how clean you are, there's going to be a little residue in your ass, and that means bacteria. You can get some really funky problems if you move from your ass to vagina. And you thought the idea of ass to mouth was gross!

YES, you can get an STD/STI from anal sex. For a long time, the AIDS/HIV problem was most often associated with the homosexual community, and it was passed on to others through anal and oral sex. Other diseases can also be passed on anally as well. So, if you aren't fluid-bonded with your husband, please use a condom for anal sex. YES, you can also get pregnant from having anal sex. If he cums in your ass, that semen won't pass through to the vagina, but if it leaks out or he pulls out as he's cumming, it's possible for some semen to end up in your vagina. While this is very unlikely, since sperm will die pretty quickly in your ass or when it hits the air, it is still possible.

Some anal lubes contain benzocaine, which is a numbing agent to help make anal sex easier. Be careful with this. You see pain is our body's way of telling us that something is wrong. I personally recommend that you use a lube that *doesn't* have benzocaine so you can tell if there's pain and fix the problem or stop the penetration until the pain subside.

Chapter 7

Getting Yourself Ready To Take A Cock

First let's try a little self-exploration.

Now that you are a little more comfortable with the fact that it's okay to be interested in anal sex you can start exploring your own ass before you let your man have at it.

If you've never had any personal experience with anyone playing with your ass before you need to explore it a bit on your own and see how it feels and get comfortable with the idea of anal play. In order to enjoy anal intercourse, you have to be able to exercise control over your mind. If you are tense, like I was when my husband and I first started out, then your asshole is going to be closed tighter than a drum and nothing will be able to penetrate it. It is incredible just how big a part your mind plays in anal intercourse. I have experienced anal intercourse on numerous occasions with my husband and have enjoyed it thoroughly. However, I have found that the times I've really enjoyed it the most have been those times where I've been the one to initiate it.

It seems to be so easy then, where on other occasions it is a bit more of a struggle to get into the right frame of mind and totally relax enough for easy penetration. So, by all means the best place to start your explorations would be of course in the bathtub. Draw yourself a nice warm bath and climb in. Alternatives would be in the shower or even just lying down on your back on your bed.

Simply take your fingers and begin running them over the insides of your thighs and all over your pussy. Try to get yourself a little worked up before you start fingering your tight little rosebud. As you become comfortable, draw your legs up toward your chest and run your fingers down your butt crack. Then rub from your pussy to your anus. See how it feels when you lightly touch your anus with your finger. Try pushing several of your fingers down against your anus. If it feels pleasurable to you, then you might want to try masturbating while your fingers are pushing down on your anus. If you find that this produces pleasurable feelings for you, or you think that it might then just keep up the exploration.

One thing you must never forget is to take it nice and slow sister, there isn't any big hurry. The rectum is similar to an elastic pipe with a set of strong muscular rings at the end, which is the anus. The anus acts as a plug, to stop things from going out or letting things that are unwanted in. It tightens and loosens like purse strings on a bag and is fairly strong. So, as you can see a woman's rectum can easily accommodate a large penis. Think about it, if the rectum can handle all your large excrement loads, then the smaller things like penises and fingers are really not a problem. The rectum is a sturdy flexible organ and isn't going to be hurt at all by fingers or a penis or any other similar object. That is unless there is intent to hurt the woman being screwed. Before inserting a finger into your anus though, please make sure that your fingernails are cut short and don't have any sharp edges as they could easily scratch or tear the tissue inside the rectum and that won't be a fun feeling at all.

While You're Carefully Exploring Your Own Ass

After some preliminary touching you will find that you want to move on and actually insert a lubed finger into your anus. At this point it is a good idea to have some good lubricant on hand. I personally would recommend a lubricant that is water soluble. I have personally used Vaseline and it is an acceptable lubricant as the rectum is a self-cleaning organism. My favorite is either a cherry flavored lube if you're doing anilingus or I D Glide anal lube.

Make yourself comfortable on your bed or whatever spot you've chosen for your passionate night of exploration and bend your legs slightly bringing your feet closer to your ass. Using one hand get into a comfortable rhythm of masturbation.

Then take a finger of the other hand, usually the index or the middle finger works best, and apply the lubricant of your choice to it. Gently start to push the tip of your finger into your anus. You will feel it give way and your finger will go in a little way. To insert the finger further you need to keep pushing gently and try to relax your anus. This will enable you to get past the thick muscle and into the rectum. This may feel a bit uncomfortable at first, and there may be a little bit of a burning sensation or irritation.

For most people this is a normal response, just try to relax your ass completely and continue the masturbation with your other hand. If you want to, sister go ahead and bring yourself to climax with your finger still in your rectum and see how it feels.

If this feels good to you, then by all means you need to continue with your self-exploration. If it doesn't feel good, then withdraw the finger and try again at another time. Take all the time you need to become comfortable with yourself being penetrated.

If you have enjoyed yourself thus far, then you might want to try wiggling your finger around inside your rectum and see what it feels like. You will soon notice that the inside of the rectum is very soft and comfy. I personally find it's a rather interesting and awesome sensation. Try moving your finger around in all kinds of different directions and see what different movements feel like to you personally.

If you have your fingers from your other hand inside your pussy, you can push them towards each other and feel them pushing on the tender walls that separate them. There is truly nothing more erotic than feeling your husbands' fingers rubbing each other from inside each place. Eventually you will want to stretch the rectum a bit more so that you can prepare it for your man's cock at a later date.

One way to do this is to try sliding another finger into your rectum to join the first one and to try spreading the fingers as far apart as you can. Only do what feels comfortable for you. Don't feel that you have to accomplish everything on the same day. You may do better if you explore a bit at a time over a span of several days, with each day going a bit further. Practice tensing and relaxing your anus around your fingers.

Okay Now You Can Use More Than Just Fingers

Now that you are starting to get comfortable with your fingers, it's time to move on to something a bit more realistic. A good hard dildo the size of your husband's penis is an excellent choice to practice with. You can obtain one at a local love shop or order one from many of the private places on the internet. I would recommend one made of plastic rather than latex to start with. Latex dildos are really difficult to clean and have soft pores that bacteria could be harbored in. Don't use anything with sharp edges or that can easily break.

On your own try inserting the dildo into your ass gradually, making sure that it is well lubricated. Try pushing it in and out of your anus while you masturbate yourself with the other hand. I have found that if I'm already excited from masturbating it is much simpler to push the dildo further into my anus without resistance.

From this point you can move on and involve your husband in the exploration process. Make sure that he is aware that you are setting the pace and not to rush the whole process. He will be greatly rewarded by the results of patience when he finally gets to experience your ass, especially if this will be a first for you.

Now You Can Let Your Lover Pistol You.

There are a couple of ways to get your partner involved in the exploration of your ass. They are pistoling and oh yes, my favorite, analingus.

Pistoling is the insertion of fingers into the anus and may involve massaging it and the inside the rectum. And in its most extreme you can end up with anal fisting, but that's a whole topic on its own. And by the way I don't recommend it.

The insertion of your lover's fingers into your anus is a great lead up to the ultimate of anal sex or it can even be a pleasant enhancement to regular intercourse. This act allows your partner to become familiar with how you may react during anal sex. It gives him a great chance to explore your body with you. This is how my husband and I started having anal sex. He would insert a lubed finger in my ass as he gripped my cunt with his fingers and pounded me with his awesome thumb. I would spray my cum everywhere. It even got to where when I'm having a hard time working up an orgasm my husband would then pistol my ass with his finger and soon, I would be blowing my load for him.

Normally, I usually find that his thick index or middle fingers work the best, being a little longer than the others and stronger as well. Please, as I've already said, don't forget the lube!

Run your fingers softly over the anal opening, kneading, and pressing against it. You can use a circular motion to do it if you like. It's just like giving a massage. You are helping the area around the anus to relax. Make the insertion by pressing gently and firmly inwards, wiggling the tip of your finger as necessary.

At this point if you're comfortable with it and relaxed enough the finger should slide in your ass fairly easily. On the other hand, if your ass is tense then your finger will not make any headway at all.

You and your partner will have to decide at this point whether or not to continue with penetration of the penis or to perhaps leave it alone and come back to it another time.

You will need to keep at least your fingertip beyond the anus, or the contraction of the muscle could just force the finger right out. When your finger is inside exploring a bit, pushing the finger as far in as it will go, flicking back and forth.

A great way to enhance this pistoling feeling would be to suck on your wife's clit or stick your other fingers in her pussy. I have found that this combination makes for some pretty powerful orgasms. There is nothing better than having his mouth wrapped around my clit and fingers wiggling in my ass. It's a great feeling.

Chapter 8

Analingus Is The Real Love Kiss

Let me say one thing from the start of this chapter before we talk about this very controversial sex act. I absolutely love to rim my husband's tender asshole and he loves to rim mine. Once while we were on vacation we got a room with a large walk-in shower, and I asked him if he wanted to get a shower with me and clean each other up really good.

When he finished cleaning up my breasts really good and making sure they were good and clean he put some soap on a washcloth and started cleaning my very private parts. After washing my pussy really good. He then went about to clean around my asshole and soon had me moaning. As he rubbed it and dabbed a finger in, he noticed me purr with each thrust, so he knew I was ready for some real ass play tonight. So, after we dried each other off he led me to the bed, and I laid down on my side and pulled my ass cheek up for him exposing my tender rosebud to him to tempt him. He placed himself behind me. After licking my clean cunt for a while to orgasm. He then had me lift one of my ass cheeks up for him with one hand and he proceeded to eat my asshole for almost an hour and two orgasms later just from eating my asshole.

So yes, he loves to rim my asshole and I love to rim his. Now let's take a little time to explore the other way to explore your spouse's rear end. This method is typically called rimming or tossing a salad but is better known as "analingus". It involves kissing, licking, and sucking on your lover's anus. Now before you say, "YUCK NO WAY" just read this whole chapter first. A lot of people have a problem with this erotic concept since we've been taught for so long that we're not supposed to play with our buttholes, because they are dirty and bad. And of course, there is the possibility of getting VD or hepatitis from an infected person. But the primary fears of rimming are mainly to do with smell, taste, and personal preference. If these things are a concern to you, then perhaps the ideal time for this sort of exploration would be right after getting out of the shower. You can also buy dams, which are made from latex, very similar to the dams they use in the dental offices, only a lot thinner.

Another trick is to use a piece of Saran wrap over the anal area before you place your tongue there. You would apply this to the area, so that you would not be coming in direct contact with your lover's ass, but they would still get all the same great sensations from your tongue.

Analingus works so well because the anus opening is so incredibly sensitive, and the lips and tongue are so warm and expressive. It's easy to do and it also can be done in any position where the buttocks can be spread far enough apart to admit the tongue. Run your tongue over the anus, licking it in soft wet strokes or circle it, running your tongue around the edge of it slowly and delicately. You can flick the tip of your tongue rapidly over the opening or try inserting your tongue as far as it will go pushing and stroking it back and forth. Try brushing your lips over the spot or sucking hard on the anus. If you are being rimmed, try to push down the anus and relax the anus as if you were shitting. It will expand a little outward giving your partner more area to caress or nibble at.

Just use your imagination and experiment a little. Just remember to always pay attention to your partner's reactions to your different amazing tongue techniques. Analingus is simply oral stimulation of the anus, more frequently referred to as "rimming." Anal has for some time been taboo in our culture, especially when it comes to sexual activity. So, in this chapter, I decided to dedicate a chapter to safely rimming because good information is what helps keep people safe, healthy, and having fun and pleasure around one of the most erotic amazing erogenous zones for both male and female alike.

Just Roll Your Tongue Around The Rim

The anus, which is the opening of the rectum, has thousands of nerve endings. This is no doubt why some people really enjoy it when their anus is stimulated by kissing, licking, or tonguing the anus. It offers a different kind of feeling than fingering or massaging. As you can imagine, because the anus is a taboo area of the body, anal play, especially as intimate as oral-anal, can be charged with sexual energy and excitement. This element alone can add to your partners' arousal and sexual enjoyment. Anal stimulation also tends to be an act that men and women both enjoy.

How To Give Your Spouse a Great Rim Job

If you and your partner decide to try rimming, please don't rush it. The anus can be a little shy at times because it sometimes constricts when it is initially stimulated. Massaging your lover's back, thighs, and buttocks can also help your partner get into the mood and relax the anus. You can also try different positions to get the best access to your lover's anus.

One of the best ways to start out is to have the receiving person lay on their stomach or get on their knees while the giver rims them from behind. It's easy to spread their ass cheeks apart in this position.

Or the receiver can straddle their partner's face and ease themselves slowly down on the giver's mouth. The giver may find that by spreading their partner's butt cheeks, they can rim deeper into their lovers anus. Each person will enjoy different types of stimulation at different times, so talk with your partner as you begin rimming them and ask them what they like and don't like. Do you enjoy me to finger your pussy while I'm rimming? Or for this lady's, do you want me to play with your balls while I'm rimming your asshole? My husband loves stimulation of the perineum which is the area between the genitals and anus. It's the root of his cock and he goes crazy when I chew on it. Try massaging their thighs or butt cheeks? Only you will know, and only you can tell your partner!

It's also okay not to want to experiment with anal play or specifically, rimming. Whether your partner wants to rim you or asks you to do this to them. Remember you can always respect their desires but also say no to engaging in anything you are not comfortable with. This does not make you a "prude." The key to a healthy, happy sex life is to engage in behaviors that make us feel good, not bad.

Chapter 9

The Best For Men Is Anal Prostate Stimulation

Anal prostate stimulation is a very hot topic these days. It has recently been featured in a lot of trending magazines marketed towards women as one of the hottest things for a woman to do in the bedroom for her man.

It has long been known that a finger in the ass during a blow job will help the guy achieve a faster, and more powerful orgasm. Recently, the popularity of these techniques has been surging. So just what is it, and why should you be willing to give it a try the next time you're going down on your man? In this chapter, you will learn several things.

The basics of anal prostate stimulation.

Why prostate stimulation feels so good.

How to start with anal prostate stimulation.

When you understand the basics of the male anatomy it will help you greatly. It will also help in learning about this very erotic technique. The male sex organs consist of three essential parts. The first, and most obvious, is of course the penis. We all know that the testicles or balls produce the sperm that comes out of the penis during ejaculation.

But most people don't realize that the prostate gland is the third part in the male orgasm equation! This gland is the size and shape of a walnut, and it also produces a man's semen, which is the fluid that combines with sperm during ejaculation. Most of a man's ejaculate is semen, and not sperm. This may be a shock to you, but it's true! That's why men tend to shoot a lot more cum during ejaculation when his prostate is stimulated. Stimulating a man's tender prostate gland is accomplished by reaching just inside the anus. The prostate gland is protected by a thin amount of tissue on the top of the anus, about one half to two inches inside. This finger stimulation will cause the prostate gland to go into overdrive and work to produce more semen. When it is being stimulated properly with a finger or prostate toy, it will feel very good for your man. This is because the majority of the good feelings he experiences during orgasm originate in the prostate.

The combination of the increased pleasure and the enhanced semen production will result in an orgasm that is very powerful. By applying some light pressure to his prostate during his orgasm, you can also really stretch out the length of his orgasm to somewhere between thirty seconds to as much as two minutes! I've left my husband just a puddle of mush lying there shaking afterwards.

So, now that you know the basics of prostate stimulation and why it feels so amazingly good for your husband. So, what can you do to get started? Most women will start out by using just their finger. This is okay, but it might also require you to have a latex glove on your hand to cover your long nails if you have them. If you have really long nails one effective technique is to put a cotton ball under your fingernail before you place the glove on your hand. Going to the drug store to purchase latex gloves and lube is definitely going to result in some weird looks. You can skip gloves, but it isn't recommended. Just go ahead and lube up their butt, slip your finger in, and see what happens. You will know as soon as you find his prostate gland, because even a light touch on it is enough to release a wave of pleasure through his cock and balls, even if he isn't hard.

The best way to get started doing this though, is with an introductory level prostate toy. These toys are available from a number of manufacturers. As a person who has tried many different brands on my man, I can confidently tell you that they are worth using.

If you are ready to move on to trying this out with your partner, then you just need to ask him if he would like you to. The prospect of experiencing an increased orgasm is great motivation for many people, and a lot of guys and girls are willing to give it at least one try. Enjoy your future pleasure with anal prostate stimulation.

You may be wondering just what are the benefits of prostate massage? The use of a prostate massager made from a medical grade nonporous plastic simultaneously massages the prostate gland and the perineum hands free via contractions of his PC muscles. This massaging effect upon the prostate gland creates rhythmic pressure, and it is this gentle pressure that stimulates the prostate, resulting in the gland swelling and producing seminal fluid.

These prostate massagers produce highly sensual pleasure sensations, especially when in combination with the massaging of the perineum, and the small cluster of nerves located between his testicles and the anus.

A prostate gland massager is also said to revive a failing male libido as the prostate gland is responsible for the flow of seminal fluid. These powerful claims have attracted thousands of men to want to try prostate massage for themselves, and many have reported favorable results. The prostate, perineum, and anal sphincter all hold important roles in the male sexual orgasms.

While you're at it why not discover prostate massage milking as well. Did you know that the prostate gland is composed of tiny structures called acini, or sacs? Over time, if you lead an unhealthy or inactive lifestyle, the fluid inside these sacs can become stagnant or unhealthy. It's at this stage that bacteria can start to grow in these sacs. If that occurs, the acini can become inflamed and swell which can result in the acini sacs closing. This is a problem because it now means bacteria can build up without any way for it to disperse.

The more acini cells that close themselves off, the more your prostate starts to swell, which leads to pain, sexual anxiety, and urinary problems. The advantage of having regular, that is weekly prostate massage milking is that the supplies the acini cells in the prostate are constantly filled with fresh new blood.

This in turn also enables you to pass on the accumulation of the seminal fluid that has been collecting in the acini cells. Giving proper prostate massage milking also helps the prostate to rid itself of harmful bacteria so that the prostate can start to heal itself. Another key benefit of the prostate massage is that it releases the seminal fluid trapped in your prostate without exercising the prostate muscles which cause ejaculation. Emptying out relieves you of the desire to ejaculate which occurs because pressure from the fluid inside your prostate gland makes you feel horny.

Your body is basically telling you it is full of cum and wants you to have sex to release it. That's great if you are into prostate massage milking for sexual pleasure, you will undoubtedly feel a very pleasant orgasmic sensation from the procedure. But if you are trying to relieve the symptoms of prostatitis and you feel a real need for sexual release, prostate massage milking can help give your prostate gland both the release and the rest it needs.

So, if you want to try your hand at prostate massage milking, the best way to do it is with an anal toy. The secret to effective prostate massage can be easily explained. The prostate gland can be a gold mine of extreme sexual thrills for those willing to carefully probe and massage it, but while all the prostate sex manuals will tell you about the medical benefits to be enjoyed from prostate massage, it is also important to understand some of the risks.

As we have already said; the prostate is that delicate gland that is responsible for most of the production of seminal fluid. It's located just under the bladder and is about the size of a walnut. It is not possible to access it directly, but it can be felt, and pressure can be applied to it through the lining of the rectal wall. As men age, the prostate gland can become subject to a buildup of bacteria and can also be susceptible to cancer. This is why doctors will check to see if the prostate is not enlarged during a medical checkup.

When prostate massage is applied for sexual pleasure, the prostate gland does swell up and produces seminal fluid, which is an exciting sexual sensation. Indeed, with practice this can lead to the male multiple orgasms. Yes, men can have multiple orgasms through prostate massage. The key to enjoying safe prostate massage is to go gently and never to rush the massage. The new generation of sex toys as we've already talked about are designed specifically to stimulate and massage the prostate safely without undue force being applied to the delicate membrane of the rectum. Correct use involves a medium to light repetitive massage or circular motion. The tool is not intended for use in a thrusting manner, but un a circular manner.

It's also important and I mean very important to apply plenty of water-based lube both to the sex toy and to the anus during the prostate massage. If you feel pain or any discomfort during the massage session, cease and consider having a medical check up to ensure all is well.

Let's Get To Giving The Prostate Massage

If you mention to most men about the concept of anything to do with anal play their reaction is not exactly that encouraging. Anything remotely sexual connected to the man's anus has been taboo for hundreds of years, even though giving a man a prostate massage actually precedes the formal establishment of acceptable sexual practices and morals in medieval times.

Generations of men have been taught incorrectly that enjoying or practicing anal sex is really bad, evil and you could even go to hell for it if you ask some people.

Unlike more everyday sexual practices such as oral sex or sexual intercourse, giving a prostate massage does require a little understanding of the male anatomy, because the prostate is not an external organ. It is located two inches inside the anus. It's a walnut sized gland located just below the bladder and is there to produce seminal fluid which helps to protect semen on its way from the penis to the vagina during ejaculation.

Pressure on this walnut sized gland through the membrane of the rectal wall can produce highly pleasurable sensations when giving the right kind of prostate massage. Push too hard or play too rough and it can be an uncomfortable, unsafe, and even a dangerous procedure. All that is required is gentle downward pressure, either with a latex gloved finger, or best of all, with a specifically designed prostate massage sex toy, which hones in on the prostate, and can at the same time, massage the highly sensitive perineum, which is a cluster of nerves located between the anus and the testicles. Always use plenty of water-based lube applied either to the gloved finger or the sex toy when giving prostate massage. That's because the anus produces no lube at all on its own. Some of the most powerful orgasms are from prostate massage. Assuming that you already have had him perform all the pre-session formalities such as urinating and having a good bowel movement. Then of course scrubbing himself nice and clean, you are now ready to prepare him for the prostate massage orgasm.

The prostate massage orgasm can be done with a lubed latex glove, but the fingers actually fall a little short of providing the best orgasm for him.

If you are then conducting prostate massage orgasm on him, first lube up your anal sex toy, or if you have not got one and don't want to order one, the next best device is just a finger. Whatever you use, because his anus produces no natural lube of its own, it needs to be properly lubed up.

The best method of entry is to have him get down on all fours and slowly insert the toy or finger into his anus. A sex toy is obviously safest and best because it is designed to massage the prostate.

Have him inhale as you insert the toy in his ass. Breathing is a very important part of prostate massage orgasm because he needs to create oxygen for the nerves you are now massaging. The prostate gland is a sensitive organ that located two inches inside towards the stomach.

If you have already carefully aroused him before starting the massage, it will be easier to find the prostate because the prostate expands when it is pleasured. You can now start to add some gentle pressure along the wall of the rectum which starts to stimulate the prostate gland. Using a downward movement, and he will start to feel the powerful sensations.

A prostate massage orgasm can be a highly sensual experience for your husband which will blow him away and at the same time prevent a buildup of semen in the prostate gland. Thus cleansing it and improving his circulation and actually making masturbation unnecessary! Always massage him gently and don't do it more than three times a week. Two times is okay but one time a week is fine.

A good way to start a prostate massage is to massage the prostate externally. Using the index and middle fingertips, you can touch, rub, stroke, or press on his perineum. Which is the area of skin from underneath the testicles between the anus. While you press on this center of nerve endings you can also stimulate other parts of his body so as to become more receptive for the actual prostate massage itself.

You should always use plenty of water-based lube for anal play, and for prostate massages. If you opt for a sex toy, you will find this much easier and more convenient to use than fingers as it is specifically designed to locate the prostate and massage it cleanly and smoothly. The combined massage of the prostate and the perineum can provide highly intense sexual sensations, and can even produce a super orgasm, akin to the multiple orgasm enjoyed by females.

An Anal Evening With Brandee Lee

I let out a sigh, as I slide my key into the lock. It had been a long day at work, and I was so sick of dealing with people for the day. I just wanted to go home, cuddle my lover, and watch some TV to chill out. My plans instantly changed when I stepped inside the house to find my husband waiting for me right at the door.

"Well, this is unexpected," I said, smiling and closing the door behind me. Instead of replying, he grabbed me and pulled me into his arms, hugging me close to him as he claimed my mouth with his. His lips were surprisingly soft, but there was an edge to his kiss that immediately made sexual heat start building in my core. He nipped at my lower lip, causing me to let out a small gasp. He immediately pressed his size advantage over me, using that opening to slide his tongue into my mouth, tasting me. He toyed lightly with the buttons on my shirt, not trying to take it off, but teasing me with additional touches before he finally grabbed my hair and broke off the passionate kiss by jerking my head back to expose my naked neck.

He kissed and bit me on the neck a few times, with each touch of his mouth making me moan louder. The heat that had been building inside my core intensified until it was positive that if he were to slip a hand up my skirt, he'd find me soaking wet.

Then, as quickly as he started revving me up, he stopped, releasing me, and turning away from me to go back into the living room. I leaned against the door for a moment, letting the cold of it stabilize me before I removed my heels. I brushed my hand down my work skirt, smoothing the lines out of it to try and regain some sense of dignity. And then I looked down at my chest, noting just how easy it would actually be to make my cleavage even more pronounced than it already was. I quickly tugged my black wrap shirt down until even I was impressed with myself.

"You're a dick honey," I said as I sat down on the far side of the couch. I made sure I was leaning forward.

He looked at me innocently as he turned on the T.V. I glared at him, debating whether I wanted to move so I could bite him. Something inside me softened as I met his gaze. I missed you too, love. "Yes." "Well then," he said, reaching out and grasping my hand. "I apologize." He brushed a kiss across my palm and then slowly down each of my fingers.

I fought hard to keep from squirming as desire once again pooled up inside of me like a fire. I reached my hand up to gently cup his face, and he again kissed my palm before meeting my gaze. This time, his eyes sparkled mischievously, but there was still an incredible tenderness in them. I settled back, and decided to watch TV with him, putting off how badly I sexually wanted him at that moment. I knew that waiting would make things even more intense, for both of us.

I stretched and let out a surprisingly sensual moan. We'd been cuddling on the couch for hours, and while I loved how gently he was caressing the special parts of my body as I lay against him, I was starting to get sleepy and relax but going to sleep was the last thing I wanted to do tonight. No, tonight was for payback. I propped myself up on my elbow and looked down at him.

Unable to help myself, I teasingly grazed my hand across his face, and then slowly traced my thumb over his lips. I then leaned down and ran the tip of my tongue across his lips before just briefly touching them with my own. Then, I pulled back and swung a leg over him, causing my skirt to ride up and reveal my naked ass as I straddled him. His eyes snapped open at that view of my butt I was giving him. And all of the interest caused him to grab a hold of my hips. I smirked and rolled my eyes as I transferred my weight to that leg and then stood up. "I'm heading to bed baby," I called over my shoulder as I shook my hair away from him. "You can stay up, though, if you'd like, but it's your loss if you do."

As I knew he would, he also instantly got to his feet, following me as I stayed just out of his reach and walked to the bedroom. Once we got into the bedroom, I was facing the bed, so I turned to face him. He reached out to touch me, but I held up a hand. He then stopped, and instead just started watching me. I ran a hand through my hair and looked up at him from under my long lashes, biting my lip at the intensity of his gaze. Then, I ever so slowly began to tug my skirt down, slowly sliding it down until the shirt was just barely still tucked into it. Then, I sensuously started running my hands up and down my sides, just barely letting my fingertips slide over soft fabric and even softer curves. I slid my index finger under the hem of my skirt, noting the way his gaze followed it as I ran it around, pulling my shirt out from under the skirt and then sliding my hands under that, revealing small glimpses of my stomach.

I suddenly changed my tactics, and then began moving my hands up my body, cupping my breasts and touching my satiny soft skin as I slipped one hand down my shirt and the other into my bra. "Oh, Brandee....." he moaned, obviously wanting to be the one touching my private parts. I didn't reply, but instead sat down on the bed and slowly began inching my skirt up my legs, revealing the bottom of my clean shaven bald pink pussy lips. I spread my legs a bit wider, and moved my hand up my skirt, lightly stroking the insides of my thighs. I didn't need to go all the way up to my pussy to know that I would find it very wet. I could feel myself aching to be filled with his meat already. Honestly, that urge hadn't gone away since the searing kiss he had greeted me at the door with.

I moved my hands back to my shirt, sliding them under it and slowly inching it off of me. I was so enjoying his rapt expression as more and more of my bare skin is slowly being revealed. When it was finally completely off, I threw it at his face. He caught it, but the distraction allowed me the time I needed to step forward and press him against the wall and kiss him deeply as he had previously done me at the door earlier. This time, I slid my tongue into his mouth, tasting him briefly before moving away and going up on my tiptoes. I lightly bit his earlobe. I softly moaned into his ear, using a breathy voice. "I'm going to make you want me so bad it hurts baby." And then I stepped back away for him.

The look of frustration and desire on his face caused me to grin a little. He stepped forward, intent to push me onto the bed and claiming me as his intension was clear on his face. But I once again held up a hand, and he stopped. He pouted, but didn't move closer, as my grin widened.

I returned my hands to myself, again roaming them over my very soft skin and curves, each time tugging at my skirt a little bit more. Finally, it slid down my legs, and I stepped out of it, noticing the way he hungrily traced my curves with his eyes.

I again sat down on the bed, and then laid on my side. As I had his total focus now, I ran my hand ever so lightly over my legs, before moving my hand further up my hip and skimming the lines of my lace black panties. As I moved my hand to caress my cunt, I rolled onto my back and spread my legs wide, allowing him to watch as I stroked my clit lightly before sliding my fingers deep inside my wet slit.

I thrust them into me only a few times before I removed my hand and lifted my glistening fingers to my mouth and sucked my wetness off of them. That time, when he moved towards me, I knew that I wouldn't be able to stop him, unless I safe worded out.

I also was so turned on I was totally fine with that and enjoyed the way he felt as he settled his hips between my legs. Even though he was still in his jeans, I could see just how aroused he was, and wrapped my legs around him, rubbing against him as much for his pleasure as for mine.

I went to hug him closer to me, and pull him down to kiss me, when he took one hand and held my wrists above my head. He thrust against me and kissed me deeply, as he used his other hand to find a pair of handcuffs in my nightstand. Once he did, he clasped my hands with them. But because we didn't have a headboard, he had nothing to cuff me to. Instead, he leaned back and said. "If you move your hands, you'll be punished babe."

I smiled, and moved my hands down just an inch, testing him. Faster than I could blink, his hands were around my wrists, squeezing just tight enough that moving would be difficult, but not enough to hurt. This is your best punishment? I thought to myself, quite amused. And then he started rubbing me through my already soaking panties. I arched my back, trying to get more of the sensation of his hands.

I yelped, flinching away from him, but his hand on my wrists held me in place. "I told you not to move."

I looked at him, my eyes now big. I was more playing at being wounded, than actually offended, but his eyes still softened. "Are you going to listen to me this time babe?" I nodded, and he removed his hand from my wrists. He kept his other hand at work, though, stroking me through my panties. He stopped long enough to remove his shirt and undo his pants, casting both to the floor amidst my own discarded clothes.

He tenderly pulled me up to him and kissed me passionately. And then he rolled in the bed, shifting it so that I was on top of him. I bit my lip and began to rock back and forth, camel toeing the hard length of him to try to satisfy my craving. I barely noticed as he undid my bra and my large tits bounced out in his face. But my attention snapped back to him when he started to suck hard on one nipple as he rolled the other one between his fingers.

I moaned, again arching my back, and rocking faster against him. The mixture of the pleasure from his hard cock and the pain on my nipples was getting me close to the edge of an amazing orgasm.

I clenched, fighting it, and then leaned forward so that I could kiss and bite his neck again. Not that he needed help getting hard, but I loved the way it made him moan.

It also allowed me an excuse to slide off of him and continue kissing my all the way down his body, stopping only to get at his jeans and slide them completely off of him. Now the both of us were only in our underwear, but I was soon to fix that, at least on his part. I continued kissing my way down his legs, and then back up again, carefully avoiding his straining member. I smiled as I saw my wet spot on his boxers where my pussy had camel toed his cock through his underwear.

I could also see it twitch through his boxers, especially when I paused to stop and put my mouth against the cock tip. We were still separated by a layer of cotton, but I could tell this was driving him crazy. I slid my slender fingers up the underside of his boxers, gently stroking his balls, but still avoiding direct contact with him.

He groaned and grabbed my hair with one hand and yanked that pesky fabric out of the way with the other. I knew he wanted to force my mouth onto his throbbing cock, but I tensed my muscles enough that he'd have a hard time pushing me down on it. However, to be perfectly honest, I was having a hard time resisting myself for he knew I loved sucking his cock. Seeing his shaft so erect, knowing just how silky soft he'd feel against my lips and down in my throat. It was all I could do to not give in to his insistent hand in my hair.

I tore my gaze away from his cock and looked at him. He was biting his lip and watching me. "Please take your hand out of my hair," I said as calmly as I could. He immediately obliged. "Sorry, I just really want to fuck your mouth like you like baby."

"I know," I replied, smiling evilly as I dropped my face down so my lips were just barely touching his cock tip. I stuck my tongue out, lightly tracing along the well-defined head of his cock. God my husband has such a beautiful cock! He flexed it, causing it to rise up just enough for me to take it into my mouth, and after that I was lost. I couldn't resist any longer.

I ran it in and out of my mouth, maintaining eye contact with him as I took it deep into my throat, and back out again. I lightly bared my teeth, using just enough to increase his sensitivity but not enough to hurt, and then stroked my tongue against his shaft. He flexed again, and seemed really close to cumming, but I wasn't about to let my fun be over that soon.

I removed my mouth and straddled him once again, feeling him wet from my mouth against my already soaking panties. Once I was again upon him, he started playing with my breasts again. I moaned, but quickly rolled off of him.

He didn't waste any time before he slid my panties off my hips and tossed them on the floor. He ran his fingers lightly against the slick wetness of my slit, just barely teasing my clit or my opening, depending on where he was. Then, he moved two fingers deep into my cunt, so quickly it almost hurt. Any pain that I might have really felt, however, was immediately cancelled out as he began stroking against my spongy g-spot softly.

I moaned, deeply low in my throat, and spread my legs wider for him to have better access to me. I wanted more, and was internally debating asking him for another finger, when I heard a buzzing. I opened my eyes to find him holding my special vibrator. He'd just turned it on, and quickly clicked through the various speeds until he found one that he liked. He pressed it against my exposed clit, and I bucked at the intense pleasure.

"Holy crap," I breathed. If he keeps that going, between the vibrations and the way his fingers were continuing to massage me, I'd cum within moments. He seemed to realize this and grinned at me before hitting a button on the wand to make it pulse. I groaned, long and hard, as I realized that he had intentionally set it in such a way that I probably would remain on the edge of an orgasm until he switched it back. "Oh, You're so evil babe."

"You still love me right," he retorted, moving his fingers out of me for a moment before adding not only another one in my pussy, but also one on my tight ass. I clenched tight, partially in surprise, but mostly in pleasure as he began to thrust his hand in and out of me. "Oh, god," I moaned deeply. He removed his pinkie finger from my ass, only to swap it out for an actual lubed up butt plug that was probably about as wide as one and a half of his fingers. He then also began to thrust it in and out of me. Adding the anal play in my ass, even with the pulsing inconsistency of the vibrator on my clit, soon brought me to the shuddering edge of an orgasm before I really realized what had happened. But he didn't stop. He kept going, and no matter how much I squirmed and screamed, the supreme waves of pleasure kept washing over me.

Suddenly, while I was still trembling from that mind-shatteringly good anal orgasm, he slid his cock deep inside of me, holding my legs up on his shoulders as he moved in and out of me. Not only did he feel incredibly large in this position, but he was also able to hit my g-spot with every stroke, which to my good only kept the orgasmic pleasure going. Somehow, he lasted a very long time, despite how fast he was pounding into me. Surprised, I looked down and realized why he was lasting so long, he was wearing a condom. Which was the first time in a long time our relationship that he'd done that. From the way he was biting his lip, though, I had the feeling that it wasn't going to be able to hold him off much longer. I squirmed out of his hands and rolled over into doggy position which is my favorite. As I did, he slipped out of me, and again, he had such a look of frustration on his face that I almost laughed. Instead, I wiggled my big ass enticingly in his face.

He smacked it with his hand, hard enough to leave a handprint. Because of the butt plug still inside my ass, it barely hurt, but instead actually felt really good. I again wiggled my butt, and he again smacked my ass. Not as hard this time, but he did continue to smack my ass, making it nice and red and warm, before I felt him pulling on the butt plug.

I pouted, though I knew he couldn't see me, but had to bite back a moan of surprise as he slid his rock-hard cock inside my tight asshole. He had no such qualms, moaning loudly and he grabbed my hips. He moved in and out at an excruciatingly slow speed and it didn't hurt at all. But every time he went in, he was able to go deeper, and I was loving every second of it. I could feel myself getting wetter and wetter and wasn't even a little surprised when I started to feel my juices running down my leg.

Instead, I just arched my big ass up to him, and rocked back and forth against him, forcing him deeper into my ass with each thrust. Then, it seemed like he had grown tired of going slow, because at that moment he grabbed my hair, pulled my head up off of the mattress, and began to slam into me, really hard and fast. I moaned loudly, uncontrollably, enjoying the feeling of him using me. He knows I love my hair to be pulled. I clenched my ass muscles, around his cock trying to make myself as tight in my ass muscles as possible for him to make it even more intense. I couldn't tell if it had helped or not, considering how much lube there was on him at this point, but it definitely made a difference for me. I could feel myself getting close to orgasm again, and it seemed like, despite the condom, he was almost ready to as well.

I reached one hand down, in between my legs. I didn't have to do more than simply touch my clit as my body rocked back and forth before and I was cumming again. He moaned my name loudly "Oh, Brandeeeeeee" and I knew he was as well, blowing a huge load in my ass. I could still feel the intensity of his release even though he was wearing a condom. I continued to squeeze my ass muscles to milk him of every last drop of cum.

Then, he let go of me, and I sank onto the bed, limp. It seemed the only thing keeping tension in my muscles before had been the desire to orgasm, but now that both he and I had done that, we were utterly spent. He withdrew from me, removed the condom, cleaned himself off, and then pulled me back against his chest, holding me tight as we fell asleep together satisfied.

Brandee Lee

Made in the USA
Las Vegas, NV
03 October 2024

96242486R00056